Altogether,
One at a Time

Also by E. L. Konigsburg

*Jennifer, Hecate, Macbeth,
William McKinley, and Me, Elizabeth*

*From the Mixed-up Files
of Mrs. Basil E. Frankweiler*

(George)

Altogether, One at a Time

A Proud Taste for Scarlet and Miniver

The Dragon in the Ghetto Caper

The Second Mrs. Gioconda

Father's Arcane Daughter

Throwing Shadows

Journey to an 800 Number

Up From Jericho Tel

Samuel Todd's Book of Great Colors

Samuel Todd's Book of Great Inventions

Amy Elizabeth Explores Bloomingdale's

T-Backs, T-Shirts, COAT, and Suit

Talk Talk

The View from Saturday

Silent to the Bone

The Outcasts of 19 Schuyler Place

*The Mysterious Edge
of the Heroic World*

Altogether,
One at a Time

e. l. konigsburg

Illustrated by

Gail E. Haley • Mercer Mayer
Gary Parker • Laurel Schindelman

Aladdin Paperbacks
New York London Toronto Sydney

ALADDIN PAPERBACKS
An imprint of Simon & Schuster Children's Publishing Division
1230 Avenue of the Americas, New York, NY 10020
Copyright © 1971 by E. L. Konigsburg
All rights reserved, including the right of reproduction
in whole or in part in any form.
ALADDIN PAPERBACKS and related logo
are registered trademarks of Simon & Schuster, Inc.
Manufactured in the United States of America
First Aladdin Paperbacks edition June 1975
Second Aladdin Paperbacks edition 1989
Third Aladdin Paperbacks edition March 2008
2 4 6 8 10 9 7 5 3
The Library of Congress has catalogued
the hardcover edition as follows:
Konigsburg, E. L.
Altogether, one at a time/E. L. Konigsburg;
illustrated by Gail E. Haley…[et. al.].
Summary: Four short stories entitled Inviting Jason,
The Night of the Leonids, Camp Fat, and Momma at the Pearly Gates.
[1. Children's stories, American. 2. Short stories.]
I. Haley, Gail E., ill. II. Title.
PZ7.K8352Al 1989
[Fic]—dc19
70-134814 CIP AC
ISBN-13: 978-0-689-20638-2 (hc.)
ISBN-10: 0-689-20638-0 (hc.)
ISBN 13: 978-1-4169-5501-6 (pbk.)
ISBN 10: 1-4169-5501-1 (pbk.)
1111 OFF

For Adolph Lobl,
with love and with memory

Contents

Inviting Jason   1

The Night of the Leonids   13

Camp Fat   29

Momma at the Pearly Gates   61

Inviting Jason

illustrated by Mercer Mayer

THE FIRST BIRTHDAY PARTY I ever had in my life was
when I was ten years old. One whole decade old.
And I had to invite Jason.

The big thing in birthday parties where we live is
slumber parties, only it isn't called a slumber party
because that's what girls call it. On the invitation
where it says FROM . . . , I wrote "Supper at 7:00
P.M., May 15." May 15 being my birthday. Where

2

it says UNTIL . . . , I wrote "After breakfast on May 16." That and the fact that I wrote at the bottom to please bring a sleeping bag lets everyone know that it is a slumber party. I had been to two slumber parties since we moved here; one of them had been Jason's.

My mother checked the invitations for spelling. When she noticed the FROM and UNTIL, she said that she had no idea that a slumber party meant a life sentence cooking and washing dishes. My mother gets sarcastic at the slightest thing. She knew that I wouldn't care if she used paper plates. Mother also noticed that Jason's name wasn't on any of the envelopes. That was besides disapproving of the way that I abbreviated Ohio. *Cleveland, Oh.* I had put. Mother said that if that was the way I abbreviated Ohio that I should use exclamation points instead of periods. Sarcastic.

"Well, where is Jason's invitation?" she asked.

"You limited me to six kids, and Jay was number seven on my list," I explained.

"Take someone off," she suggested, the way an umpire *suggests* to a batter that he's out.

I took off John Beecham; he was the only one I had invited who I didn't really like. I had added him even though he hadn't invited me to his party. Dick

3

liked him. Dick was the fastest runner in the fourth grade and the second fastest in the whole school. As a matter of fact, if Dick couldn't make it on May 15, I would have to change the date. I thought about it again and decided that I ought to have John Beecham to give Dick something extra to come for.

"I don't think Jason can come," I told Mother. "He has dyslexia."

"It's not contagious," Mother said. "Invite him," she added.

I forgot that Mother would know what dyslexia was. She had explained it to me in the first place. Mother is big on education. Dyslexia has to do with education, or at least reading. If you have dyslexia it's like your brain is a faulty TV set; the picture comes through the wires all right, but some of the tubes are missing or are in the wrong places. So that when you tune in to one channel you may get the sound from another. Or spots of the picture may be missing or be backwards or upside down. Kids with dyslexia read funny.

Jason used to read funny in class until they discovered that he had it. Then they quit making him read out loud and sent him down to special reading during our regular reading. They also sent him down during our P.E., P.E. being physical education. And it was too bad about that; Jason could handle a ball like there was nothing wrong with him. But his reading was like the Comedy Hour; that's about how long it took. Except that Mrs. Carpenter wouldn't let us laugh. And when Jay was called to the board to write something, it was like he was writing sideways, and that took three hundred hours.

Jason's mother, Mrs. Rabner, told Mother that he had improved a lot since he had been tutored in dyslexia. The nicest thing about Jason was his mother. She did everything she could to make my mother and me feel welcome when we moved here in September. But we had moved around enough for me to know that your first friends aren't always your best friends.

I ripped up the envelope that had John Beecham's address and addressed the last one to Jason Rabner. The invitations came eight in a package, but I had ruined one envelope spelling *boulevard* wrong. I had thought that spelling everything out and writing in ink made it look more important. After two bad mistakes of which I could fix only one, I wrote the rest in pencil instead of ink and abbreviated everything I could, including *Ohio*.

Inviting Jason was a mistake from before the time the party began because that's when he arrived.

5

Fifteen minutes before. I didn't like the idea of everyone else arriving and Jay looking buddy-buddy with me like some cousin or brother-in-law.

Mother served fried chicken, and the only person with a real appetite was Jason. He ate thirds. Everyone else was anxious to get on with the party and stopped at seconds. Jason cleared his plate and carried it to the sink where Mother was standing. She said, "Thank you, Jay; you're a real gentleman." No one else took the hint. I looked at Dick and rolled my eyes to the top of my head long enough for him to get the message but not long enough for Mother to get it, too.

When it was time to blow out the candles, Jason sang Happy Birthday with such concentration that when he got to Happy Birthday, dear Stanley—Stanley being my name—his *St* wet the icing and everyone kind of picked at the cake. Except, of

course, Jason, who ate his all gone. I caught Dick's eye again.

The first thing we did after eating was to get on with the party. I had opened each present as it arrived so that there didn't have to be any grand opening; I don't think that that is bad manners. Just girls (mothers) think so.

Our first game was a drawing contest to see who could draw the best. We drew girls. With their clothes off. Grown-up girls. We passed the pictures all around. Since it was my party, I got to be judge.

Dick held on to Jason's picture for a long time before passing it back to me for judging. There was something sort of spooky about it. I awarded Dick first prize; his drawing was neat, and I decided that neatness counts. We crunched the pictures up and put them in the garbage can right after.

Next we sat around on the floor and played cards.
Jason made a real fool of himself. He wanted to lose.
He kept throwing down his cards and saying things
like "Gol dang it, I thought I had him." A measly
pair of fours. Then old Jason would throw in his
M & M's. That's what we were playing for—the
M & M candies that Mother had put in our party
cups. Jay had only about ten brown ones left, and
they were worth the least. Dick had cashed in a red
for five brown and had bid three brown plus one
yellow when Mother broke up the game. I told her
that it wasn't for money. True, but it *was* gambling.

8

Also true. It was also messy. Someone had stepped on my winnings.

"Bed time," she said.

We pushed back all the furniture in the den and laid out the sleeping bags. Now was the time for ghost stories, but the truth is that no one could tell a ghost story and tell it right. They were all full of *uh's* and *and's* and they never told them in order. We told jokes full of swear words; I told one that I had heard my father tell the man from the office who he had brought to the house for supper. Everyone laughed. I was relieved because if someone had asked me to explain it, I would have had to fake it. But they either understood or else no one wanted to be the one to ask.

Mom and Dad took turns coming in to tell us to quiet down and go to sleep. Jason was the first to konk out; at least he didn't snore. It wasn't long before it was morning and everyone was ready for breakfast.

Everyone was more ready than Mother was. She put on a bright dress and make-up, but I knew what was going on underneath both.

Mother made bacon and eggs and put out two different kinds of cold cereal and orange juice and told everyone to pick up a plate and serve himself.

9

We almost ran out of bacon after Jason filled his plate. Almost. Mother told everyone to roll his sleeping bag and gather up his belongings and then play outside until he got picked up.

One by one they left. Two called their mothers to remind them. Jason sure didn't call his mother. Dick's mother had called us to tell us that she would be late picking up Dick since she had a beauty parlor appointment every Saturday; she said she would stop by for him on her way home, if that would be all right with us. I took that call, and I said that that would be fine with us.

By that time, it would have been nice if Jason's mother would come for him so that I could have some time alone with Dick. I guess she wasn't anxious to get him back, either. I had to help Mother push the den furniture back in place, and Dick and Jay were looking through LIFE magazines while I did that.

When I finished, I asked Jay if he would like to call his mother. "I'll dial it for you," I suggested. Jason did not look enthusiastic. After I finished that call, Jay and Dick were still sitting together. Jason had one of the pads we had drawn our girl pictures on last night. He was writing something when his mother arrived. I carried his sleeping bag out for him, meeting Mrs. Rabner halfway up the walk. I figured there was no point in having her come in. All she'd do would be to have coffee with Mother, and Jay would hang around for that.

Dick said goodbye to Jason and said, "I enjoyed talking with you." Dick also said "See ya" to him.

Jason said goodbye and thanked both me and my mother for the party. At last he was gone. I said to Dick, "Too bad about Jay." Saying that allowed room for Dick to say the first bad thing.

Dick said, "You know, dyslexia makes things come out different. Like I read him the story about the astronauts and here is how he wrote it." I looked at what Jay had written:

> *They nogged down and stepped onto the*
> *glans. Nothing looked farc wol, so*
> *Allen lo men . . .*

"He sure can't spell," I said.

Dick glanced over the paragraph again. "The way he writes seems better for the moon than what the magazine said."

"That's one way of looking at it."

"Yeah," Dick added. "And here's a picture I asked him to draw. Doesn't it look kind of the way that moon pictures should?"

"Maybe," I said, "but it sure don't rate hanging in any museum."

"No *earth* museum," Dick explained. And then Dick said three more nice things about Jason.

When Dick's mother came for him, I had had enough of the party. Mother made me help her load the empty Coke bottles into the car. "Aren't you glad that you asked Jason, after all?" she asked.

I answered, "No!"

Which was the same answer I would have given before the party, and I would have meant it just as much. Only my reasons would have been different.

The Night of the Leonids

illustrated by Laurel Schindelman

I ARRIVED AT Grandmother's house in a taxi. I had
my usual three suitcases, one for my pillow and my
coin collection. The doorman helped me take the
suitcases up, and I helped him; I held the elevator
button so that the door wouldn't close on him while
he loaded them on and off. Grandmother's new
maid let me in. She was younger and fatter than the

new maid was the last time. She told me that I should unpack and that Grandmother would be home shortly.

Grandmother doesn't take me everywhere she goes and I don't take her everywhere I go;

but we get along pretty well, Grandmother and I.

She doesn't have any pets, and I don't have any other grandmothers, so I stay with her whenever my mother and my father go abroad; they send me post cards.

15

My friend Clarence has the opposite: three Eiffels and two Coliseums. My mother and my father are very touched that I save their post cards. I also think that it is very nice of me.

I had finished unpacking, and I was wondering why Grandmother didn't wait for me. After all, I am her only grandchild, and I am named Lewis. Lewis was the name of one of her husbands, the one who was my grandfather. Grandmother came home as I was on my way to the kitchen to see if the new maid believed in eating between meals better than the last new maid did.

"Hello, Lewis," Grandmother said.

"Hello, Grandmother," I replied. Sometimes we

talk like that, plain talk. Grandmother leaned over for me to kiss her cheek. Neither one of us adores slobbering, or even likes it.

"Are you ready?" I asked.

"Just as soon as I get out of this girdle and these high heels," she answered.

"Take off your hat, too, while you're at it," I suggested. "I'll set things up awhile."

Grandmother joined me in the library.

I have taught her double solitaire, fish, cheat, and casino. She has taught me gin rummy; we mostly play gin rummy.

The maid served us supper on trays in the library so that we could watch the news on color TV. Grandmother has only one color TV set, so we watch her programs on Mondays, Wednesdays, Fridays and every other Sunday; we watch mine on Tuesdays, Thursdays, Saturdays and the leftover Sundays. I thought that she could have given me *every* Sunday since I am her only grandchild and I am named Lewis, but Grandmother said, "Share and share alike." And we do. And we get along pretty well, Grandmother and I.

After the news and after supper Grandmother decided to read the newspaper; it is delivered before breakfast but she only reads the ads then. Grandmother sat on the sofa, held the newspaper at the end of her arm, then she squinted and then she tilted her head back and farther back so that all you could see were nostrils, and then she called, "Lewis, Lewis, please bring me my glasses."

I knew she would.

I had to look for them. I always have to look for them. They have pale blue frames and are shaped like sideways commas, and they are never where she thinks they are or where I think they should be: *on the nose of her head*. You should see her trying to dial the telephone without her glasses. She practically stands in the next room and points her finger, and she still gets wrong numbers. I only know that in case of fire, I'll make the call.

I found her glasses. Grandmother began reading messages from the paper as if she were sending telegrams. It is one of her habits I wonder about; I wonder if she does it even when I'm not there. "Commissioner of Parks invites everyone to Central Park tonight," she read.

"What for?" I asked. "A mass mugging?"

"No. Something else."

"What else?"

"Something special."

I waited for what was a good pause before I asked, "What special?"

Grandmother waited for a good pause before she answered, "Something spectacular," not even bothering to look up from the newspaper.

I paused. Grandmother paused. I paused. Grandmother paused. I paused, I paused, I paused, and I won. Grandmother spoke first. "A spectacular show of stars," she said.

"Movie stars or rock and roll?" I inquired politely.

"Star stars," she answered.

"You mean like the sky is full of?"

"Yes, I mean like the sky is full of."

"You mean that the Commissioner of Parks has invited everyone out just to enjoy the night environment?" We were studying environment in our school.

"Not any night environment. Tonight there will be a shower of stars."

"Like a rain shower?" I asked.

"More like a thunderstorm."

"Stars falling like rain can be very dangerous and pollute our environment besides." We were also studying pollution of the environment in our school.

"No, they won't pollute our environment," Grandmother said.

"How do you know?" I asked.

"Because they will burn up before they fall all the way down. Surely you must realize that," she added.

I didn't answer.

"You must realize that they always protect astronauts from burning up on their reentry into the earth's atmosphere."

I didn't answer.

"They give the astronauts a heat shield. Otherwise they'd burn up."

I didn't answer.

"The stars don't have one. A heat shield, that is."

I didn't answer.

"That's why the stars burn up. They don't have a shield. Of course, they aren't really stars, either. They are Leonids."

Then I answered.

"Why don't you tell me about the shower of stars that isn't really a shower and isn't really stars?" She wanted to explain about them. I could tell. That's why I asked.

Grandmother likes to be listened to. That's one reason why she explains things. She prefers being listened to when she *tells* things: like get my elbow off the table and pick up my feet when I walk. She would tell me things like that all day if I would listen all day. When she *explains,* I listen. I sit close and listen close, and that makes her feel like a regular grandmother. She likes that, and sometimes so do I. That's one reason why we get along pretty well.

Grandmother explained about the Leonids.

The Leonids are trash that falls from the comet

called Temple-Tuttle. Comets go around the sun just as the planet Earth does. But not quite just like the planet Earth. Comets don't make regular circles around the sun. They loop around the sun, and they leak. Loop and leak. Loop and leak. The parts that leak are called the tail. The path that Earth takes around the sun and the path that Temple-Tuttle takes around the sun were about to cross each other. Parts of the tail would get caught in the earth's atmosphere and light up as they burn up as they fall down. Little bits at a time. A hundred little bits at a time. A thousand little bits at a time. A million bits.

The parts that burn up look like falling stars. That is why Grandmother and the Commissioner of Parks called it a Shower of Stars. The falling stars from Temple-Tuttle are called the Leonids. Leonids happen only once every thirty-three and one-third

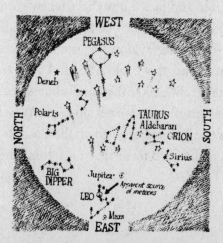

years. The whole sky over the city would light up with them. The reason that everyone was invited to the park was so that we city people could see a big piece of sky instead of just a hallway of sky between the buildings.

It would be an upside-down Grand Canyon of fireworks.

I decided that we ought to go. Grandmother felt the same way I did. Maybe even more so.

Right after we decided to go, Grandmother made me go to bed. She said that I should be rested and that she would wake me in plenty of time to get dressed and walk to Central Park. She promised to wake me at eleven o'clock.

And I believed her.

I believed her.

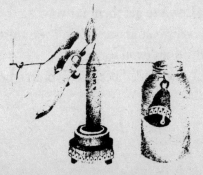

I really did believe her.

Grandmother said to me, "Do you think that I want to miss something that happens only three times in one century?"

"Didn't you see it last time?" I asked. After all, there was a Shower of Leonids thirty-three and one-third years ago when she was only thirty, and I'll bet there was no one making her go to bed.

"No, I didn't see it last time," she said.

"What was the matter? Didn't the Commissioner of Parks invite you?"

"No, that was not the matter."

"Why didn't you see it then?"

"Because," she explained.

"Because you forgot your glasses and you didn't have Lewis, Lewis to get them for you?"

"I didn't even wear glasses when I was thirty."

"Then why didn't you see it?"

"Because," she said, "because I didn't bother to

find out about it, and I lost my chance."

I said, "Oh." I went to bed. I knew about lost chances.

Grandmother woke me. She made me bundle up. She was bundled, too. She looked sixty-three years lumpy. I knew that she wouldn't like it if I expressed an opinion, so I didn't. Somehow.

We left the apartment.

We found the place in the park. The only part that wasn't crowded was up. Which was all right because that was where the action would be.

The shower of stars was to begin in forty-five minutes.

We waited.
And waited.

And saw.

"What are you crying about?" Grandmother asked. Not kindly.

"I have to wait thirty-three and one-third years before I can see a big spectacular Shower of Stars.

26

I'll be forty-three before I can ever see a Leonid."

"Oh, shut up!" Grandmother said. Not kindly.

"I'll be *middle-aged*."

"What was that for?" I asked. "What did I do?" I asked. "What did I do?" I asked again. I had always thought that we got along pretty well, my grandmother and I.

27

"You add it up," Grandmother said. Not kindly.

So I did. I added it up. Sixty-three and thirty-three don't add up to another chance.

I held Grandmother's hand on the way back to her apartment. She let me even though neither one of us adores handholding. I held the hand that hit me.

Camp Fat

illustrated by Gary Parker

Our camp had an Indian name just like every other camp in the mountains, but we called it Camp Fat. And so did every other camp in the mountains.

Sarah was going to music camp. Linda to arts and crafts, Gloria was going to science camp and Fay to water sports. When they asked me where I was going, I told them *regular camp*. Sarah said that she didn't believe me, and Linda said that she didn't either because there was no such thing as regular camp. I asked them where they thought regular kids went, and they said that regular kids didn't ever go to camp.

The day I left, my mother said, "Clara, inside every fat little girl, there is a skinny little girl screaming to get out."

And I said, "Inside this fat little girl, there is a skinny little girl screaming, 'I'm hungry!'"

They sent me anyway. Camp To Ke Ro No. Camp Fat.

The first thing they tell you after they take away all your money so that you can't buy snacks even if they had a snack bar, the first thing they tell you is that being fat isn't healthy. Miss Coolidge, who is in charge of Camp Fat, also tells you that you'll like yourself much better if you're thin. I liked myself enough already. My trouble was that I especially liked myself well-fed.

They had an assembly for the parents, too. Here Miss Coolidge told them how Camp Fat was going to make us lovely and healthy. They added the *lovely* for the parents. They showed slides of kids before and after camp. The whole program was like a long commercial for Diet Pepsi, so I watched the audience; it was easy to see where a lot of baby fat comes from.

At the first weigh-in all you're allowed to wear is a towel. I took a very small one. It is more embarrassing, but it weighs less. If you've been fat as long as I have, you've learned a thing or two. Some kids who had been to Camp Fat for three years in a row didn't know that. My goal was to lose fifteen pounds in six weeks. That's a lot for a kid.

All of our counsellors were middle-aged and muscular except Miss Natasha. Miss Natasha came only at night; she came to our cabin only on Friday night. That first Friday, I had been lying in bed thinking that if they didn't put something chocolate on the menu soon, I was going to either foam at the mouth or kick the cook some place indecent, when this pinpoint of light came waving through the darkness. It stopped at Christy Long's bed. Christy had been crying again. And don't think that listening to her helped anything. Of course, Christy had two reasons to cry; she was supposed to stop sucking her thumb besides stop eating. Miss Coolidge had promised to work on the crying the next year.

Miss Natasha's light didn't stop at every bed. She came to mine right after Christy's. She introduced herself.

"That's a weird name," I said. "Really weird."

"It's Russian," she answered.

"Well, you guys sure didn't make it to the moon first," I said.

"You mean the moon moon?" she asked.

"Yeah, like up-in-the-sky moon. How come you don't know?"

"Oh," she said, "I don't think about things like that very much. I hardly think big at all. I think little."

"I thought that Miss Coolidge would want you to think thin."

"Oh, yes, that, too," she said. "That's why I'm here. To help you to think thin. Do you wish to have dialogue?"

"If it's chocolate covered and has three scoops of whipped cream," I answered.

"When I ask you if you wish to have dialogue, it means, do you wish to talk, back and forth, with me?"

"You want me to talk?"

"Yes. Tell me what you're thinking, and then I can tell you what I think of what you're thinking, and so on."

"First of all, I'm thinking that I would like to run a fever, a fever of about one hundred and eighteen degrees. They'd get me out of here pretty fast then."

Miss Natasha said, "I really thought that since you were awake, you would want to talk. Otherwise, I wouldn't have bothered to come tonight."

"What kind of dialogue did you have with Christy Long?" I asked. I didn't wait for Miss Natasha to answer because I wanted to tell her something else that I was thinking: "That Christy is one kid I'm sure going to show to my parents. She makes me look good. She's not only fat and sucks her thumb but she also cries a whole lot. The next one I'm going to show my mother is Linda Stark. She has pimples and picks her nose besides being fat." Miss Natasha didn't say anything, so I continued with some of that week's thinking. "Do you realize that the two Robins in our cabin weigh more than the three Lindas in Cabin Twelve? Robins! Their mothers should have named them Pelicans or Ostriches. Probably Pelican would be best because neither one of them can run worth a darn. Kim is the worst brat, though. She's only plump, so she acts like she's Miss Universe. She says that she has a glandular imbalance. Ha!" That was all I said to Miss Natasha. I had run out of dialogue.

Miss Natasha waited. When I didn't add anything else, she said, "Well, Clara, that's a start. Not an especially good one, but a start." And then she patted the blanket over my knee. As she did so, the ring that she wore on the little finger of her left hand, a plain looking gold dome ring, sprang open. I lifted her hand that had the ring, and it was the most beautiful watch I have ever seen.

Miss Natasha focussed her flashlight on it. The

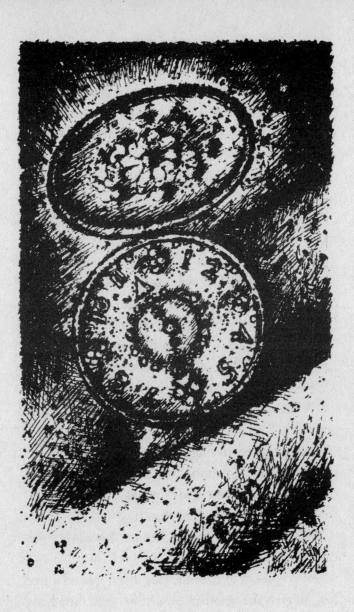

face of the watch was a thin layer of mother-of-pearl, and the numbers that weren't actual numbers were tiny jewelled flowers. That's why the lid was domed so that they wouldn't get mashed. The hands seemed to float to the proper time.

"Oh," I said, "I thought that that was just a plain old ring."

"Yes," Miss Natasha said, "It looks plain, but I made it open easily."

"You made it?"

"Yes, I made it. That was my work long ago."

"In Russia? I thought that Communists don't like fancy watches or people to wear them."

"When I lived in Russia, there was not only a shop for fancy things like this but also a very fancy king and queen who bought many of them."

"What was the matter with this one? Couldn't you sell it?"

"I never tried. I couldn't take the things that I made out of the country when I left. Except one thing. I made this watch in America."

"It sure doesn't look like what it is."

"Yes. It looks plain, but, you see, I made it open easily."

She was about to close the ring again when I asked her to give me another look. She held her hand close under my face and focused the light on it again. I put my ear to it and heard the faintest whir. A tiny whir. "Is it a Swiss watch movement?" I asked.

"No, Timex," she laughed. And then she closed the top dome over the watch. Miss Natasha checked the other beds quickly but did not stop at any others. She must have gone on to the next cabin. I fell asleep right after she left.

We had to jog to breakfast every day. It was never anything worth running for. You just had to run— one of the rules. You would think that Camp Fat would be the cheapest camp in the nation. They spent practically nothing on food and absolutely nothing on chocolate.

We had to write home every Sunday.

Dear Mom and Dad,
   This is number one letter and you are lucky I have the strength to write it.
                        Clara

At our first weekly weigh-in I had starved off fourteen pounds, but the scale said two. Liar. Even the kids who had lost more than average didn't get any reward. Like chocolate.

Miss Natasha didn't come again until the next Friday night. I guessed that that was her night for our cabin. I was figuring out how I could manage a convulsion while I was waiting in line at the next weigh-in. I had just decided that I would throw myself on the floor, jerk my arms and legs around and mutter "chocolate, chocolate," when I saw Miss Natasha's light. She stopped at Christy's bed again. Christy had made progress; now she cried silently and only sucked her thumb between meals. Miss Natasha stayed at Christy's bed a long time. Then she flashed her pinpoint of light on this bed and that on her way to me. Everyone was either asleep or pretending, so mine was the next bed she stopped at.

"Do you wish to have dialogue?" she asked.

"Only if it's about French fried potatoes or cheeseburgers," I answered.

Miss Natasha laughed and sat on the edge of my bed. She put her flashlight into her lap and her hands on either side and leaned back, stretching her neck.

"Where's your ring?" I asked.

38

"I chose not to wear it this evening," she said.

"That's too bad," I said. "I thought we could dialogue about it."

"Not tonight. Is there anything else you'd like to talk about?"

"Frozen custard." I answered.

"Well, goodnight then," Miss Natasha said. She leaned over as if she were going to kiss me.

"Don't you dare kiss me," I hissed. "My overweight is due to a severe disease which is extremely contagious. One kiss from me, and you'll be fat all the rest of your entire life."

"Really?"

"Yes," I told her. "The State Department is thinking of sending me to India and Biafra to kiss all the kids there to fatten them up, but my mother and father are extremely prejudiced and besides, my dad is not sure that the trip is tax deductible."

"Well," Miss Natasha said, "I was leaning over only to straighten your pillow."

"You can do that," I said.

She didn't move.

"You may do it now," I said.

As she leaned over, I started saying, "At the moment I am very busy making a list of people that I am very personally going to kiss and give . . ." I

39

noticed a locket dangling from a chain around Miss Natasha's neck. The locket was shaped like a teardrop and was no bigger than a Tootsie Pop; on the front cover was a scene of children wearing wreaths of flowers on their heads and dancing in a circle. Miss Natasha leaned forward so that I could examine it better. It looked like a locket, but I couldn't find any way to open it.

"What's the matter with this thing? Is it some kind of phony locket?" I asked.

"No," Miss Natasha said, "I don't make phony jewels. It has had an accident. Look on the back of it."

I did. The whole back of the locket was cracked and chipped. It must have been beautiful before it was broken. All green and gold. "Can't it open at all now?" I asked.

"Yes, it can. But it is very difficult."

"Why don't you fix it?"

"I did the best I can."

I looked down at her hands and this time I noticed that her knuckles were all swollen, and her fingers looked like someone had once taken them off and reattached them at crazy angles. Funny that I hadn't noticed them when I had seen the ring. I guessed that I had been too busy looking at the ring. "You got arthritis or something?" I asked.

"Yes," she answered.

"Do you take aspirin for it? Aspirin is supposed to be good for the minor pains of arthritis and other stuff."

"I'm afraid that I'm beyond taking aspirin," Miss Natasha said. "If you care to try to get the locket open, I think that you'll find that it is worth the effort. I was furious when it was damaged, but then I realized that nothing was coming out of my fury, so I repaired it as best I could. There is something very beautiful about having this locket work in spite of its being hurt."

All the time that she was talking about being beautiful and hurt, I was trying to get it open. Miss Natasha had been leaning forward and holding her flashlight so that I could work it. "Did Christy see this?"

"Yes."

"Did she get it open?"

"No. She couldn't. I tried to help her, though. But she couldn't get it open yet."

"No wonder it's so hard for me. Her spit from sucking her thumb is probably all over it, making it icky for me." Most of the trouble, though, was that the repair work had hidden the hinge, and I couldn't find whichways it opened. Finally, I did. And it did.

"Those are the same tiny children pictured on the

outside," I said.

Miss Natasha smiled and nodded yes.

"Why they're jewelled and gorgeous enough to make every Barbie doll in the country want to barf from jealousy. Tiny princes and princesses no bigger than peeled pistachios."

"Can you find the ring, on the top of the maypole?" Miss Natasha asked.

I did.

"Pull it."

I did. The tiny, jewelled children started swinging around the pole, and chimes played a pretty tune.

"Au Clair de la Lune," Miss Natasha said. *"In the Moonlight.* That's the name of the song. Doesn't that fit?" she asked looking out the window.

"I guess I would say that it does," I admitted. "Is this a Swiss movement?" I asked.

"No, Walt Disney," she laughed. Then she snapped closed the beautiful locket.

"It sure closes easier than it opens," I said.

"Most things do," she answered. And then Miss Natasha left my bed and left our cabin.

How they could expect all that fresh air and exercise to do anything but make me more hungry, I'll never know. At our next weigh-in, I had lost a total of five pounds. That's a lot for a kid, but according to them, I was just on schedule. Five pounds every two weeks.

We had to write home again:

Dear Mom and Dad,

I feel so nauseous all the time that I would throw up if I had anything to.

Clara

I thought that maybe Miss Natasha was coming on some other night of the week, too, and that I was missing her because I was so sleepy from starvation and exhaustion. I waited for her to appear on Tuesday, Wednesday and Thursday, but she didn't come. When she finally did come on Friday night, I asked her, "You sure don't do much work around here. Don't you think it would be cheaper for Miss Coolidge to have a record player playing 'think thin' under our pillows?"

"But a record player can't talk back," she said, "or show you this." Miss Natasha held out her hand.

In it was the ugliest, smelliest looking blob that I had ever seen in my life. There were no words to describe it, so I said, "Yicchh."

She didn't say anything, so I asked, "Did you damage this one, too?"

"In a way, I did. I was trying to preserve what is in here. Inside here is the only thing that I was allowed to bring out of my country when I left. I should have known better than to think that adding layers of plastic could preserve all of my fine workmanship. A plain, simple but strong exterior would have been better."

"It stinks. It sure smells rotten. Is that Christy's spit?"

"No. Christy is still working on the locket. You see, the plastics that they had when I left my country were not nearly as refined as they are now. This is celluloid, and it is discolored by light, and it smells so bad because it once caught on fire. Well, actually, I tried to burn off the plastic, but I found that the whole thing was in danger of melting. There is nothing to do but to chip it away. Very carefully. A little bit at a time."

"Yicchh," I explained. Miss Natasha continued holding her blob. "I don't think that I want to bother with it," I added.

45

"Most people don't want to," she said.

"Are you sure that Christy's spit isn't on it?"

"I'm sure," she said. "It's messy to get all the way through to the good parts, but it's worth it."

"Why don't you peel away all the gunk by yourself?"

"It is very difficult for me."

"Because of your arthritis?"

"Partly. And partly because I am not always sure that it is worth the trouble."

"Hunh! You just told me that it was worth it. Just this minute you told me that."

"But, of course, I can tell you that because for you it is. You are young, and you will have almost your whole life to enjoy what you will find inside. I have none of that anymore."

"Do you mean that when I get to what is inside that," I said, pointing to her blob, "that you will give it to me? Is that what you mean when you say that I will have my whole life to enjoy it?"

"No. That isn't what I meant. What I have inside here is too valuable for me to give you. I can only let you see it. What do you think I am? A fairy godmother?"

"And what do you think I am? Your mother's helper, Cinderella? Do you expect me to do all that work just to get a look at what's inside?"

"That's what you expect of everyone you meet," she said. "You expect everyone to see what is inside all that fat of yours. And not everyone can take the time. But you can. You have the time."

"Well, I'm not about to do all the work," I told her.

"Even though you'll have the image of what is inside with you for all the rest of your life?"

At that point in the dialogue I zonked my head to one side on the pillow and pretended that I had suddenly fallen asleep. Miss Natasha picked up her blob and walked out. She didn't even bother flashing her light on the other beds. She sure didn't earn her pay, I thought. Dialoguing with only two kids in a whole cabin. One stupid Friday night a week.

I had lost three pounds at the next weigh-in. It was really three and one-fourth, but Miss Coolidge said that ounces don't count. Miss Coolidge is as narrow-minded as her skinny hips.

Dear Mom and Dad,

Next weekend is Parents Visiting Day. Don't expect a Miss America.

Cordially,

Clara

Well, my parents came to Parents Visiting Day. They always like to see if they are getting their money's worth. To show them how lucky they were to have me for a daughter, I showed them two Lindas and one of the Robins. Also Christy Long. I noticed Christy showing me to her mother.

I looked all over for Miss Natasha, but she wasn't there. I even bothered to ask Christy if she had seen her today, and Christy took her thumb out of her mouth long enough to say that she had not.

Some parents must have brought some kids some goodies, which the weigh-in the next Monday showed up. Miss Coolidge shook her narrow head, clicked her thin tongue and said to every single girl who didn't lose any weight or who didn't lose enough, "Did Santa Claus come to you early this year?" She said it to each one. Including Kim. Ha. Ha.

I waited up for Miss Natasha on Friday, and after she finished with Christy, I pretended that I was asleep. Who was she that she should think that I would wait up for her? She sat on the edge of my bed, and I noticed that she was holding her blob. It wasn't hard to notice; it stunk as bad as ever.

48

"Aren't you even going to ask if I want dialogue?"

"Don't you?"

"All I want to know is why you didn't show up on Parents Visiting Day."

"I'll show up when they have Parents Visiting *Night*."

"Do you still want me to peel that gunk for you?" I asked.

"No," she said, "I want you to peel it for you."

"Aha!" I said. "You mean that you've thought it over, and you are going to give it to me after all."

"I told you that I am no fairy godmother. I do want you to work on it. It is worth it. But you must believe that yourself."

"Will you help?" I asked.

"I've already helped as much as I can."

I picked up Miss Natasha's smelly old blob and began prodding it with my finger. "You know," I said, "you ought to bring the watch so that I can keep track of the time and you ought to bring the locket so that I can listen to it as I work on this."

"I'll bring them. I'm glad you like them so much. As a matter of fact, I have to go back to Christy's bed to get the locket. She's still working on it. Now you must start alone. I'll be back shortly."

"Why don't you just leave it in my little old shop

here, ma'am. I'll give you a claim check, and I'll call you when it's done."

"Clara," Miss Natasha said, "if you had all day to do it, you'd put it off and put it off, and it would never get done."

So I began the gruesome job, letting my mind wander. Miss Natasha returned to my bed and watched me work a little while longer before she picked up her blob and walked out. I had gotten so interested in picking away at that mess that I forgot that she had the locket on when she had returned from Christy's bed. I was sorry that I missed another chance to see and hear it.

Dear Mom and Dad,

Only three things make me sick anymore. Kim, all the push-ups over 15, and the goop they call boiled cabbage.

Fondly,
Clara

I had decided to be friendly; that's why I signed it *Fondly*.

Even the smell of Miss Natasha's burnt plastic ball
didn't bother me anymore. Maybe because I was so
close to the end and there wasn't much of it left.
Maybe because Miss Natasha brought the ring and
the locket now and that helped to take my mind off
it.

I finished on the last Friday before I went home.
The week before the plastic coat had gotten so thin
that I was able to see what was inside. It was gold
and the size of an airmail stamp. I peeled away the
last of the plastic and saw that the gold was a tiny
book whose cover was jewelled and locked.

"I'll bet it is a miniature Bible," I said.

Miss Natasha was as anxious as I was to get to it.
"Open it! Open it!" she urged.

I did.

Oh,
my pretty

Oh,
my Clara

Oh,

my pretty

Oh,
my love.

"Oh. Ohhhhhhh! Oh. Ohhh," I repeated, which is not at all like me. "I know now that you are going to give it to me, after all. That *is* me. That's a thin Clara. You made it just for me, didn't you?" I looked up at Miss Natasha with grateful tears in my eyes, which is also not at all like me. "You put all that mess on it so that I would have to realize that I'm not plain on the outside like the watch and I'm not damaged like the locket. I'm fat and a little nasty and have to take all that off by myself so that people can see the beauty inside. I know now, dear Miss Natasha, that you are going to give me the tiny gold book, the greatest treasure of them all."

"No, I am not," Miss Natasha said. "I told you that I'm no fairy godmother. Make your own pictures." And with that, Miss Natasha took the book from me and left.

When my parents came to take me home from camp, I could tell that they were pleased with the way I looked, so I said, "I need new clothes. Nothing fits."

They had another assembly for parents to tell them about how they should help us by making only skinny suppers and by not having a lot of snacks except cottage cheese and carrots around the house.

57

I looked for Miss Natasha at the assembly. I wanted to say a different goodbye to her. I couldn't find her.

After the assembly broke up, I separated from my parents and found Christy Long to ask her if she had seen Miss Natasha, and she hadn't either. There was nothing to do but to ask Miss Coolidge. I should have written my parents that Miss Coolidge was the fourth thing that made me sick. I thought that my mother and father ought to meet Miss Natasha. And I did owe her another goodbye, a better goodbye. I asked Miss Coolidge if she had seen Miss Natasha.

"Miss Who?" she asked.

"Miss Natasha, the evening counsellor," I said.

"We have no Miss Natasha," Miss Coolidge said. "As a matter of fact, we have no evening counsellor."

I looked at Miss Coolidge. She was skinny. Her legs were skinny. Her elbows were skinny. Her brain was skinny. I stared into her skinny eyes.

"Miss Natasha, you say?" she said. "Years ago, Camp To Ke Ro No was an Arts and Crafts camp, and we had someone here named Miss Natasha. She taught jewelry making. She claimed that she used to work for the royal Russian court."

"Where do you think she is now?" I asked.

"Oh, she's dead. She died. As a matter of fact, it

58

was after she died that our arts and crafts enrollment went down so badly that we had to change the camp. If Miss Natasha were still with us, we never would have gone into the beef business."

It wasn't because Miss Coolidge called me beef that I knew that I would never return to Camp Fat, and it wasn't because she told me Miss Natasha was dead that I knew that I would never return to Camp Fat. It was because of Miss Natasha that I knew that I would never *need* to.

Momma at the Pearly Gates

illustrated by Gail E. Haley

My momma tells about the time that she got bused. She lived in a town in Ohio that year, and everybody walked to school except Momma who took a bus. And everybody went home for lunch in that town in that year except Momma, and that, too, was because she took a bus.

The reason that Momma was being bused was because of Mrs. Clark, who was her teacher. One of her teachers. When Momma's folks moved from one part of town to the other, Mrs. Clark said that she thought that it would be a shame for all of Momma's smarts to go down to that other school with all the poor colored kids. Of course, Momma was poor at that time, too, and she was as black then as she is now (Momma and I are just about as black as each other), but Mrs. Clark thought that it would be better for Momma to stay put for the rest of the school year. Mrs. Clark spoke to the school principal and got special permission for Momma to stay at Franklin School where everyone appreciated her.

That's how Momma came to take the city bus to school everyday. Her folks bought her a book of bus tickets, costing four cents a ride. She carried her lunch to Franklin School everyday, and Momma never minded. She knew that she was loved.

When I ask Momma what it was like back in those days, she tells me that they didn't have TV. Well, I know that! She tells me that they had radios but the radios were mostly pieces of furniture that you kept at home and not transistors that you carried around with you. When I ask her what else, she says that a lot more white people were poor then.

When I try to picture Momma in those days

she says that I am all wrong. And when I try again,

she says that I am still wrong and that I should remember that she was, after all, a city child.

Then she says, "Does knowing that we had saddle shoes and zippers help any?" And I tell her, yes, it helps.

I mentioned that Mrs. Clark was only one of Momma's teachers. The other was Miss Mayer. Each one of them taught fifth grade. Everyone liked Mrs. Clark better than Miss Mayer. Miss Mayer had been to Europe twice, so she taught geography and history to both fifth grades and Mrs. Clark taught English and arithmetic to both. The kids stayed in the same room, and the teachers moved back and forth across the hall. Now, all that shows what the difference was between those times and these.

1. Nowadays, geography and history are called social studies.

2. Nowadays, sharing teachers is called team teaching.

3. Nowadays, I have already had three teachers who have been to Europe, and I am only in the fifth grade, too.

4. Nowadays, they make the kids and not the teachers change classes.

Momma had been busing for two weeks, being all alone in the Franklin School during lunch hour and enjoying it. She visited the first grade room where they had white lines painted on the top of the blackboard all around the room. In that room there were big pieces of chalk which Momma was afraid to use and small pieces which she was not. She practiced making the beautiful alphabet and got so that she could write just like it.

Two days the weather was nice, and she sat on the down end of a seesaw and ate her lunch. All alone, and proud to be it.

Momma says that the blackboards at the Franklin School were the most beautiful she has ever seen. As a matter of fact, she says that that is the first time she ever thought black is beautiful. The blackboards were real slate and high, so high that only Mrs. Clark who was very tall could reach the top edge. The blackboards in the Franklin School went all around the room—except on the side where there were windows. The windows, too, were tall, so tall that they had to be opened and closed with a pole. Momma says that when the sun came in at the window, it glared on part of the front blackboard and that then you couldn't see what was written there. Mrs. Clark or Miss Mayer would move to the side and everyone would twist around in his seat because the seats were bolted to the floor. You could keep track of the seasons by watching how late in the day

the sun glared on the front left part of the blackboard.

Momma says that there was a blackboard even in
the back part of the room, and I say that that blackboard must have been pretty useless, what with no
one being able to turn his seat around, what with
them being bolted to the floor. Momma says that
the blackboard in the back of the room turned out to
be the least useless one. When I ask her what she
means by that, she says she'll come to it, and kids
today are always too frantic to get to the end. When
Momma says "kids today" she always just means
me.

When Momma visits my school, she looks at our
blackboards—and then she looks at me with pity.

After Momma had been bused for two weeks, Roseann Dolores Sansevino began carrying her lunch to school. She was in the fourth grade and walked to school and walked home. She was considered responsible, so she was allowed to carry her lunch. For some reason she had to. When I ask Momma why Roseann Dolores Sansevino couldn't go home for lunch, Momma says that people didn't ask so many questions in those days.

Miss Thompson, the fourth grade teacher, brought Roseann up to Mrs. Clark's room so that the girls could eat together. Roseann had long braids, each one as thick as her wrist and the ends of them were curled below the rubber bands. She held her eyes down shyly as Miss Thompson introduced them to each other. Then they were left alone in Mrs. Clark's room.

"What did you bring for lunch?" Momma asked.

Roseann Dolores Sansevino said, "Shut up, you dirty nigger."

Momma went up to Roseann, grabbed one braid in one hand and the other in the other, jerked first one and then the other and said, "Ding Dong Dago."

And even then Momma didn't shut up as Roseann had told her to. She went to Mrs. Clark's desk and sat at it and unwrapped her lunch, scrunching the waxed paper. Momma says that there wasn't any plastic wrap or Baggies then. She had a peanut butter and jelly sandwich; she chomped it. Then she sat back in Mrs. Clark's chair and sucked peanut butter out of her teeth as much as she could. And as loud as she could. Momma says that in those days the peanut butter was always oily at the top when

you bought it, and the first sandwiches were oily
and the last ones were dry. That day her sandwich
had been from the bottom and was on white bread,
besides. Momma says that those were two-gallon
sandwiches because that's how much water it took to
wash them off the roof of your mouth.

Roseann looked out the window and would only
now and then turn in Momma's direction, and when
she did, it was to look disgusted. Momma got up
from Mrs. Clark's chair and walked to the door and
said, "If you need me for anything, I'll be in the
teachers' lounge."

Momma says that in those days no one was ever
allowed in the teachers' lounge. No one even deliv-
ering a message to someone in the teachers' lounge
was allowed in; the message was shoved under the
door. Momma says that teachers used to not be allowed to smoke cigarettes, and so they hid when
they did.

Momma didn't know that the teachers' lounge
would be locked even during lunch hour. When she
found out that it was, she went into the third grade
classroom across the hall and waited. She decided to
wait long enough for Roseann to get the idea that she
had completed her business. As she sat in that third
grade room, in the back, away from the door, she

noticed on the back blackboard

The *please do not erase* was so that the janitors would not wash it off when they cleaned the room at night.

Momma was studying that map when she heard footsteps down the hall. She stayed very still and heard someone jiggle the door to the teachers' lounge, then more footsteps heading back toward Mrs. Clark's room. Momma waited about five minutes more, and then she headed back toward Mrs. Clark's room.

"Was that you trying the door while I was in the teachers' lounge?" she asked.

"So what if it was?" Roseann replied.

"Door knob jiggling won't get you through the door of the teachers' lounge any more than it will get you through the Pearly Gates of Heaven."

"I bet there's no niggers in Heaven," Roseann said.

"What's the matter with you?" Momma asked. "Haven't you ever heard of Nigger Heaven? The way I hear white folks talk about it, that's the best part of Heaven to go to. It's full of bright colors, watermelon and gambling. And all there is in your Heaven is harp music and praying."

"What's wrong with that?"

"Nothing's wrong with that," Momma said, "especially if you'd rather have harp music and praying than watermelon and gambling."

"I'm going down to my room," is all that Roseann would say.

And Momma shrugged, "You can go down farther than that for all I care."

The next day Miss Thompson brought Roseann up to Mrs. Clark's room again. This time Miss Thompson said, "Roseann thought it would be a good idea if you ate in our room today. That way, each of you would be hostess every other day." So Momma and Roseann walked down to Miss Thompson's room. Momma took a look at Roseann's face and didn't like what she saw. When I ask Momma what it was that she saw there, she says *satisfaction*.

After Miss Thompson left Roseann picked up her lunch and parked herself behind Miss Thompson's desk. She unwrapped her sandwiches and began chomping on them.

Momma said to her, "Do you know what you're doing?"

Roseann said, "Only the same thing that you did yesterday."

73

And Momma said, "That's right, honey. That's what you're doing. You're imitating a nigger."

They finished their lunch in silence before Momma said, "I'm going down to first grade to practice."

Roseann didn't say anything, but after about five minutes, she followed Momma down there and watched Momma practice the beautiful handwriting.

Momma was hostess the next day. Roseann came up without Miss Thompson. She sat in the back of the room, and Momma sat at Mrs. Clark's desk. Neither of them said a thing. Momma began to hum and glance through some books that were on the edge of Mrs. Clark's desk. She stopped humming, closed the book hard, and said, "Well, I've got to get to work."

She picked up a piece of chalk from the top of Mrs. Clark's desk, a long, new piece, and marched to the blackboard, the useless one, in the back of the room. And she began to draw.

Roseann Dolores Sansevino said, "I know how to draw a fish without once lifting my chalk from the board."

"If you want to do that kind of baby stuff, take the baby pieces of broken chalk and do it over there,"

Momma said, pointing to the blackboard on the side of the room.

So Roseann worked on the side blackboard and Momma filled the back.

Both of them erased both boards clean before even the first person returned from lunch.

The next day when Roseann was hostess in Miss Thompson's room, Momma finished eating and then said, "Well, I'm going back up. I've got work to do."

She began drawing on the back blackboard again.

When Roseann came in, Momma glanced her way and continued with her work. Roseann scribbled and doodled and erased what she did right after she did it. But not Momma. Momma was involved in a project.

Roseann stopped working at her own board and began to watch Momma. Lunch hour was almost over. Momma stood back from her work, and she knew that she couldn't bear to erase it. So she walked back to the blackboard and wrote:

*Please
do not
Erase!*

exactly like the writing on the first grade blackboard.
And also like Miss Mayer's handwriting.

Miss Mayer thought that the work belonged to
Mrs. Clark and Mrs. Clark thought that the work
belonged to Miss Mayer. Mrs. Clark would never
scold Miss Mayer for using up her blackboard be-
cause everyone liked Mrs. Clark better and Mrs.
Clark knew it, so she was always very polite to Miss
Mayer. Anyway, Momma's work was not erased.
Just as Momma had planned.

The next day Momma got to work right after
eating and Roseann Dolores Sansevino watched.

The next day Momma finished.

Roseann Dolores Sansevino watched again.

"How come you colored in all their faces?" Roseann asked.

"Because they are black people," Momma said.

"Noah wasn't any nigger," Roseann said.

"I didn't say he was. I said that he was black."

"Ha!" Roseann said, "Then why did you color
them in white?"

"Because that is the way you show a black Noah
on a blackboard. Black and white is how you look
at things. I think that this is the way that Noah
should look on blackboards. And I think that this is
the way he will look in Nigger Heaven."

"You fresh thing, you," Roseann said. "I'm going to tell Mrs. Clark and Miss Thompson and Miss Mayer that it's you who's been drawing on the blackboard."

Momma said, "You go right ahead."

Roseann did. She waited in the classroom, glaring at Momma, until Mrs. Clark returned from lunch. Mrs. Clark was hardly in the room real good before Roseann called out, "Look what *she* did!" She pointed to Momma's work.

Mrs. Clark smiled at Momma and said, "Did you really do that?"

Momma nodded yes.

"Well, that is wonderful. Just wonderful." She turned to Roseann and said, "Thank you for telling me." Then she picked up Roseann's hand and said, "Let's go down and tell Miss Thompson together."

That must have been when Miss Thompson and Mrs. Clark arranged for the fourth grade class to come up and see what Momma had done because they were only about three problems into their arithmetic lesson when the fourth grade marched in.

Mrs. Clark was proud to introduce Momma to the fourth grade and Momma was proud to stand and take credit. Everyone said, "Gollee" and "Gosh." Momma says that kids didn't say "Cool" or "Neat" back then. The one thing they kept saying was, "Did you really? Did you really do it?"

Momma nodded yes. And then yes again. And she smiled, smiled, smiled.

78

The kids kept asking, "Did you really do it?"

And that was when Roseann Dolores Sansevino said, "She really did it. I watched her from start to finish." She said it loud enough for everyone in the whole fourth and fifth grades to hear.

Momma says that this time, the time that she was bused, was the beginning of two things. Well, Momma is an artist now; she draws the pictures for stories like this one, and she has even won a medal for it. And this time, the time that she was bused, was the beginning of it.

When I asked Momma, "What is the other thing it was the beginning of?"

Momma says that the other thing is told in the story.

Here's a excerpt from the latest
stunning novel by E. L. Konigsburg

the
mysterious
edge of the
heroic world

IN THE LATE AFTERNOON ON THE SECOND FRIDAY IN September, Amedeo Kaplan stepped down from the school bus into a cloud of winged insects. He waved his hand in front of his face only to find that the flies silently landed on the back of his hand and stayed there. They didn't budge, and they didn't bite. They were as lazy as the afternoon. Amedeo looked closely. They were not lazy. They were preoccupied. They were coupling, mating on the wing, and when they landed, they stayed connected, end to end. They were shameless. He waved his hands and shook his arms, but nothing could interrupt them.

He stopped, unhooked his backpack, and laid it on the sidewalk. Fascinated by their silence and persistence, he knelt down to watch them. Close examination revealed an elongated body covered with black wings; end to end, they were no longer than half an inch. The heads were red, the size of a pin. There was a longer one and a shorter one, and from what he remembered of nature studies, their size determined their sex—or vice versa.

The flies covered his arms like body hair. He started scraping them off and was startled to hear a voice behind him say, "Lovebugs."

He turned around and recognized William Wilcox.

William (!) Wilcox (!).

For the first time in his life Amedeo was dealing with being the new kid in school, the new kid in town, and finding out that neither made him special. Quite the opposite. Being new was generic at Lancaster Middle School. The school itself didn't start until sixth grade, so every single one of his fellow sixth graders was a new kid in school, and being new was also common because St. Malo was home to a lot of navy families, so for some of the kids at Lancaster Middle School, this was the third time they were the new kid in town. The navy seemed to move families to any town that had water nearby—a river, a lake, a pond, or even high humidity—so coming from a famous port city like New York added nothing to his interest quotient.

Amedeo was beginning to think that he had been conscripted into AA. Aloners Anonymous. No one at Lancaster Middle School knew or cared that he was new, that he was from New York, that he was Amedeo Kaplan.

But now William (!) Wilcox (!) had noticed him.

William Wilcox was anything but anonymous. He was not so much alone as aloof. In a school as variegated as an argyle sock, William Wilcox was not part of the pattern. Blond though he was, he was a dark thread on the edge. He was all edges. He had a self-assurance that inspired awe or fear or both.

Everyone seemed to know who William Wilcox was and that he had a story.

∽◦ ◦∽

Sometime after William Wilcox's father died, his mother got into the business of managing estate sales. She took charge of selling off the contents of houses of people who had died or who were moving or downsizing or had some other need to dispossess themselves of the things they owned. She was paid a commission on every item that was sold. It was a good business for someone like Mrs. Wilcox, who had no money to invest in inventory but who had the time and the talent to learn a trade. Mrs. Wilcox was fortunate that two antique dealers, Bertram Grover and Ray Porterfield, took her under their wings and started her on a career path.

From the start, William worked side by side with his mother.

In their first major estate sale, the Birchfields', Mrs. Wilcox found a four-panel silk screen wrapped in an old blanket in the back of a bedroom closet. It was slightly faded but had no tears or stains, and she could tell immediately that it had been had painted a very long time ago. She priced the screen reasonably at one hundred twenty-five dollars but could not interest anyone in buying it. Her instincts told her it was something fine, so when she was finishing the sale and still couldn't find a buyer, she deducted the full price from her sales commission and took the screen home, put it up in front of the sofa in their living room, and studied it. Each of the four panels told part of the story of how women washed and wove silk. The more she studied and researched, the more she became convinced that the screen was not only very fine but rare.

On the weekend following the Birchfield sale, she and William packed the screen into the family station wagon and tried selling it to antique shops all over St. Malo. When she could not interest anyone in buying it, she and William took to the road, and on several consecutive weekends, they stopped at antique shops in towns along the interstate, both to the north and south of St. Malo.

They could not find a buyer.

Without his mother's knowing, William took

photos of the screen and secretly carried them with him when his sixth-grade class took a spring trip to Washington, D.C. As his classmates were touring the National Air and Space Museum, William stole away to the Freer Gallery of Art, part of the Smithsonian that specializes in Asian art and antiquities.

Once there, William approached the receptionist's desk and asked to see the curator in charge of ancient Chinese art. The woman behind the desk asked, "Now, what business would you be having with the curator of Chinese art?" When William realized that the woman was not taking him seriously, he took out the photographs he had of the screen and lined them up at the edge of the desk so that they faced her. William could tell that the woman had no idea what she was seeing, let alone the value of it. She tried stalling him by saying that the curatorial staff was quite busy. William knew that he did not have much time before his sixth-grade class would miss him. He coolly assessed the situation: He was a sixth grader with no credentials, little time, and an enormous need. He squared his shoulders and thickened his Southern accent to heavy sweet cream and said, "Back to home, we have a expression, ma'am."

"What's that?" she asked.

"Why, back to home we always say that there's

some folk who don't know that they're through the swinging doors of opportunity until they've got swat on their backside."

William waited.

It may have been because he returned each of her cold stares with cool dignity, or it may simply have been the quiet assurance in his voice coupled with his courtly manners that made it happen, but the receptionist picked up the phone and called the curator, a Mrs. Fortinbras.

William showed Mrs. Fortinbras the photographs, and Mrs. Fortinbras was not at all dismissive. She said that the photographs—crude as they were— made it difficult to tell enough about the screen. But they did show that it might be *interesting*. She suggested that William bring the screen itself to Washington so that she could arrange to have it examined by her staff.

When school was out for the summer, William convinced his mother to pack up the screen again and drive to Washington, D.C., and have Mrs. Fortinbras and her staff at the Freer give it a good look.

And they did take it there.

And Mrs. Fortinbras and her staff did examine it.

And Mrs. Fortinbras and her staff did recommend that the museum buy it.

And the museum did buy it.

For twenty thousand dollars.

When they got back to St. Malo, William called the newspaper. The *Vindicator* printed William's story along with the pictures he had taken. The article appeared below the fold on the first page of the second section.

⁕ ⁕

William was now standing above Amedeo as he crouched over his backpack. Taking a minute to catch his breath, Amedeo examined the lovebugs on the back of his hand and asked, "Do they bite?" He had already witnessed that they did not.

"They're harmless," William said. "They don't sting or bite."

"Are they a Florida thing?"

"Southern."

"I haven't ever seen them before."

"They swarm twice a year. Spring and fall."

Amedeo pointed to one pair that had just landed on his arm. "Is that all they do?"

"From about ten in the morning until dusk." William raised his shoulder slowly and tilted his head slightly—like a conversational semicolon—before continuing. "The females live only two or three days. They die after their mating flight."

Amedeo laughed. "Way to go!"

William smiled.

Amedeo picked up his backpack and started walking with William.

"Do you live here?" Amedeo asked.

"No."

"Then why did you get off at my stop?"

William's smile faded. "I didn't know it was your stop. I thought it was a bus stop."

"I meant that I live here. So it's my stop."

"I'm not gonna take it away from you," William replied, and his smile disappeared.

They had reached the edge of Mrs. Zender's property. Without a whistle or a wave, William headed down the driveway.

Amedeo stopped to watch.

William lifted the back hatch of a station wagon that was parked at the bottom of Mrs. Zender's driveway. No one who lived on Mandarin Road owned a station wagon. Mrs. Zender drove a pink Thunderbird convertible: stick shift, whitewall tires, and a car horn that pealed out the first four notes of Beethoven's Fifth Symphony.

Amedeo watched as William removed a large brown paper bag from the back. It was not a Bloomingdale's Big Brown Bag, but a no-handles, flat-bottom brown bag from a grocery store. He could tell from the way William lifted it that the bag was definitely not empty. He carried the bag up to Mrs. Zender's front door and walked right in without ringing or knocking. He knew that he was being watched, but he did not once look back.

Amedeo waited until William closed the door behind him before he walked down the driveway himself.

Amedeo had been inside Mrs. Zender's house once. Two days after moving to St. Malo, they still didn't have a phone, and his mother had sent him next door to ask the lady of the house permission to use her phone to "light a fire" under them. *Them* being the phone enemy.

Amedeo's mother was an executive with Infinitel, an independent long-distance telephone company that was a competitor to Teletron, St. Malo's communications provider. To his mother, the telephone was as vital a connection as the muscle that connected her hand to her arm. If St. Malo already had had access to cell phones, she wouldn't be in this predicament, but then if St. Malo already had access to cell phones, they wouldn't be in St. Malo at all. The only thing neutralizing her indignation about not having a working phone was the embarrassment the local company was suffering at not being able to properly service one of their own. But on this morning there was also the pool man (whom she secretly believed to be the one who had cut the line) to deal with. She chose to wait for the pool man herself and to send Amedeo next door to deal with the phone. Amedeo had been happy to go.

A wide threshold of broken flagstones led to the front door of Mrs. Zender's house. There were no torn papers and dried leaves blowing up against a ripped screen door as in the opening credits of a horror movie. Her grounds were not littered with papers but with pinecones and needles, fallen Spanish moss, and big leathery sycamore leaves. Her lawn was cut but not manicured; her shrubs were not pruned, and except for the holes through the branches that the electric company made to protect the wires, her trees were wild. The paint on her front door was peeling. Her place looked shabby. Shabby in a genteel way, as if the people who lived there didn't have to keep up with the Joneses because they themselves *were* the Joneses.

Amedeo wiped a moustache of sweat from his upper lip with the sleeve of his T-shirt. Like a performer ready to go on stage, he stood on the threshold and took a long sip of the hot, moist gaseous matter that St. Malo called air. He lifted his hand to ring the bell.

The door swung wide, and the entire opening filled, top to bottom, with a sleeve. The sleeve of a silk kimono. "Yes?" the woman said, smiling. Her smile engaged her whole face. Her mouth opened high and wide; her nostrils flared, and her eyebrows lifted to meet a narrow margin of blond hair. Just beyond the hairline, her head was covered by a long, gauzy silk scarf—purple—that was tied in an elaborate knot below her left ear but was still long enough to hang to her waist. She wore three shades of eye shadow—one of which was purple—and heavy black mascara. Her lips were painted a bright crimson, which feathered above and below the line of her lips and left red runes on three of her front teeth.

It was nine o'clock in the morning.

Amedeo had never seen anyone dressed like that except when he was in an audience.

"Hello," he said. "My name is Amedeo Kaplan, and I would like permission to use your phone."

Mrs. Zender introduced herself and commented, "Amedeo. Lovely name."

"Thank you. People usually call me Deo."

"I won't," she said. "*Amedeo* is Italian for *Amadeus*, which means 'love of God.' It was Mozart's middle name."

"It was my grandfather's first name. I'm named for him."

"Lovely," she said, "lovely name, but how did you get here, Amedeo?"

"I walked."

"You walked? From where?"

"From next door."

"Oh," Mrs. Zender replied. "I didn't know there was a child."

"There definitely was. *Is.*"

"I didn't know."

"I was at camp."

"Music camp?" Mrs. Zender asked.

She smiled expectantly, waiting for an explanation. Fascinated, Amedeo watched her upper lip squeegee away one of the red runes. When he didn't answer, she told Amedeo to follow her, and with a sweep of sleeve, she pointed the way. The underarm seam of her kimono was split. Mrs. Zender was not a natural blonde.

As they traveled the distance of a long center hall, they passed two or three rooms so dark it was hard to tell where one ended and another began.

Every window was covered with heavy drapes, which dropped from padded valances. The word *portière* from *Gone With the Wind* came to mind.

In several windows, the drapes had been shortened to accommodate a bulky window air conditioner that was noisily waging war with the heat and humidity. And losing. They passed a dining room large enough to be a ballroom. In the semi-light, Amedeo could make out a *Phantom of the Opera* chandelier hanging over a table that looked long enough to seat the guest list at Buckingham Palace. Opposite the dining room was a room with a baby grand piano; its open lid reflected the few slits of light that pierced the parting of the drapes. The dark-ness and the drawn drapes added a dimension to the heat. It was August. It was St. Malo. It was hot. Hot, hot, hot.

But the thickness of the air carried the sound of music—opera—out of the rooms and transformed the hallway into a concert hall. Amedeo slowed down and cocked his head to listen.

Mrs. Zender said, "So you like my sound system."

"Definitely."

"One of a kind," she said, "Karl Eisenhuth himself installed it."

"Karl Eisenhuth? I'm sorry, I don't know him."

"Then I shall tell you. Karl Eisenhuth was the world's greatest acoustician. He had never before installed a sound system in a private home. He had done opera houses in Brno and Vienna and a symphony hall in Amsterdam. Mr. Zender, my late husband, contacted him and requested that he install a sound system here. Karl Eisenhuth asked Mr. Zender why he should bother with a private home in St. Malo, Florida, and Mr. Zender replied with three words: *Aida Lily Tull*. That was my professional name. Those three words, *Aida Lily Tull*, were reason enough."

Amedeo said, "I'm impressed." He was.

Mrs. Zender said, "I'm pleased that you are."

And for reasons he did not yet understand, Amedeo was pleased to have pleased.

Mrs. Zender swept her arm in the direction of the back of the house. The hallway was wide enough to allow them to walk side by side, but Mrs. Zender walked ahead. She was tall, and she was zaftig. Definitely zaftig. She was also majestic. She moved forward like a queen vessel plowing still waters. Her kimono corrugated as she moved. There was a thin stripe of purple that winked as it appeared and then disappeared in a fold of fabric at her waist.

Amedeo was wearing a short-sleeved T-shirt and

shorts, but the air inside the house was as thick as motor oil, and perspiration soon coated his arms and legs and made his clothes stick like cuticle. Mrs. Zender seemed not to be sweating. Maybe she followed the dress code of the desert and insulated herself with layers of clothing. Arabs and motor oil had been in the news a lot lately.

The combination of heat, music, and the mesmerizing rock-and-roll of Mrs. Zender's hips made Amedeo worry about falling unconscious before reaching the door at the end of the hall. What were the names of clothes that desert people wore? *Burnoose . . . chador . . . chador.* His mother did not approve of chadors.

The rock-and-roll stopped when Mrs. Zender arrived at the door at the end of the hall. She waited for Amedeo to catch up, and then with a flutter of sleeve and a swirl of pattern, she lifted her right arm and pushed the door open. For a minute, she stood against the door, her arm stretched out like a semaphore, beckoning Amedeo to pass in front of her.

He walked into the kitchen, and Mrs. Zender quickly closed the door behind her.

The music stopped.

An air conditioner was propped into the kitchen window and was loudly battling the throbbing pulse of heat that bore into the room. Like his house, Mrs. Zender's faced east. By August, the afternoon sun was too high to make a direct hit on the kitchen windows, but was still strong enough to bounce off the river and push yellow bands of heat through each of the slats of the Venetian blinds.

The kitchen itself was a time capsule. The counters were edged in ribbed chrome and topped with pink patterned Formica that was peeling at the seams. Near the sink sat a set of metal cylinders labeled FLOUR, SUGAR, COFFEE. There was a toaster oven, but no microwave. The stove was the width of two regular stoves, eight burners, two regular ovens, and a warming oven. It was gleaming bright, clean, and obviously had not been used in a very long time. It would take courage to turn it on. Cold cereal and vichyssoise would be better menu choices.

On the countertop in the corner of the kitchen near the dining alcove, there was a small telephone. Turquoise. Rotary dial. Not touch-tone. Amedeo had seen people in the movies use a rotary phone, and he knew the phrase "dial a number," but he had never done it.

Mrs. Zender said, "That's a princess phone."

"Does it work?"

"Of course it works. Except for my cleaning

service, which is not here today, everything in this house works."

Amedeo lifted the receiver. The part of the phone he held to his ear had yellowed from turquoise to a shade of institutional green.

Mrs. Zender sat at the kitchen table. Amedeo felt he was being watched. He turned to face the wall of cabinets.

The cabinets reached to the ceiling. It would take a ladder to reach the top shelves. The cabinet doors were glass, and Amedeo could see stacks and stacks of dishes and matching cups hanging from hooks. Behind other glass doors there were platoons of canned soups—mostly tomato—and a regiment of cereal boxes—mostly bran. Everything was orderly, but the dishes on the topmost shelves were dusty, and the stemware was cloudy, settled in rows like stalagmites.

Finally, he heard, "Your call may be monitored for quality assurance," and was told to listen carefully "to the following options." He realized that he could not exercise any of the "following options." He could hardly press one or two when there were no buttons to press. He held his hand over the mouthpiece and whispered, "I'm supposed to push one for English."

Mrs. Zender smiled wide. The last of the red runes had been washed away. "Do nothing," she said. "Just hang on. When you have a dial phone, they have to do the work for you." She threw her head back and laughed.

Amedeo didn't turn his back on her again.

As soon as the call was finished, they returned to the long, dark hall, where the heat and the music swallowed them. Mrs. Zender paused to say, "I suppose you put central air-conditioning into your place."

Amedeo hesitated. Until that moment, he had never thought of central air-conditioning as something a person put in. He thought it came with the walls and roof. "I suppose so," he said.

"Sissies," Mrs. Zender said. Then she laughed again. She had a musical laugh. "I chose a sound system over air-conditioning."

"But," Amedeo replied, "I think you're allowed to have both."

"No," she said crisply. "Karl Eisenhuth is as dead as my husband."

"Oh, I'm sorry."

"Yes, a pity. There never will be another sound system like this one."

Reluctantly, Amedeo left Mrs. Zender, her veils, her house.

❧ ❧

Now, Amedeo watched William walk through that peeling, painted front door without stopping or knocking and enter Mrs. Zender's world of sound and shadow.

From 2-time Newbery Medalist
E. L. Konigsburg

*The Outcasts Of
19 Schuyler Place*
0-689-86637-2

*From the Mixed-up Files of
Mrs. Basil E. Frankweiler*
NEWBERY MEDAL WINNER
0-689-71181-6

The View from Saturday
NEWBERY MEDAL WINNER
0-689-81721-5

*Jennifer, Hecate, Macbeth,
William McKinley, and Me, Elizabeth*
NEWBERY HONOR BOOK
0-689-84625-8

Altogether, One at a Time
0-689-71290-1

The Dragon in the Ghetto Caper
0-689-82328-2

Father's Arcane Daughter
0-689-82680-X

Journey to an 800 Number
0-689-82679-6

*A Proud Taste for Scarlet
and Miniver*
0-689-84624-X

The Second Mrs. Gioconda
0-689-82121-2

Throwing Shadows
0-689-82120-4

Silent to the Bone
0-689-83602-3

Aladdin Paperbacks • Simon & Schuster Children's Publishing
www.SimonSaysKids.com